Walt Disney's

Goofy
and the
Magic Fish

 Book Eight

Disney PRESS

New York

Adapted from *Goofy and the Magic Fish*,
illustrated by Angel Rodriguez and Ivan Boix

Printed in China

First Edition
1 3 5 7 9 10 8 6 4 2

ISBN 978-1-4231-4895-1
T425-2382-5-11129

For more Disney Press fun,
visit www.disneybooks.com

ONCE UPON A TIME, there lived a fisherman named
Goofy. Goofy had everything he could ever need:
a house by the shore, a little rowboat, and some
fishing nets. But he was bored.

Every morning Goofy rowed out to sea in his little boat. He threw his net into the water. When he pulled it back in, it was full of fish. Goofy put the fish in a bucket and threw his net back into the water. He did this over and over. When Goofy had filled his bucket with

fish, he rowed home again. As night fell, he ate his dinner and went to bed. In the morning, he started all over again.

Then one morning, something very strange happened. Goofy tried to pull in his net, but it wouldn't budge. He tugged and tugged. Finally he yanked the net into his boat. In it was the biggest fish Goofy had ever seen!

Just then the fish began to talk. "Listen carefully, Goofy," it said. "I am a magic fish, and magic fish do not taste good. Throw me back in the water, and I will give you anything you wish for!"

Goofy gladly threw the fish back in the water. He had never seen a talking fish before, and he was terrified! But he did have a wish.

"I wish I were a farmer," Goofy said. "Fishing is such boring work. I'm sure that farming would be more exciting."

Poof!

Suddenly Goofy found himself standing on a small farm. There were cows in a field. Ducks swam around in a small pond, and chickens pecked at the ground.

"What an amazing fish," Goofy said, looking around. "Yes, I think I'll enjoy being a farmer."

But Goofy did not enjoy farming. It was more exciting than fishing, but there was also more to do. There was so much work. The cows had to be milked. The fields had to be plowed. And the pigs and chickens had to be fed.

Every time Goofy thought he had finished his work, the animals made a new mess. The pigs got into his garden and ate his apples. A cow wandered away and got lost in the cornfields. The chickens got loose and knocked over the bucket of milk Goofy had just finished filling. And some rabbits ran away with his carrots!

By the end of the day, Goofy was exhausted! He was too tired to fix the broken fence or chase the crows away from his garden. He was even too tired to wonder how his wheelbarrow had ended up *on top* of a haystack! He slumped down against a fence and tried not to fall asleep. Being a farmer was too much work!

Then Goofy remembered the magic fish.

Goofy hurried down to the beach. He got into his rowboat and paddled out to sea.

"Magic fish! Magic fish!" he called. "Come up and help your poor friend."

Soon the magic fish appeared. "Are you back so soon?" it asked.

"Being a farmer is too hard. I wish I were a sea captain!" said Goofy. "I'm sure that would be easier."

Poof!

Without another word, Goofy found himself standing on a beautiful boat. It was loaded with goods, and Goofy had a crew of men to do all of his work for him.

"What an amazing fish," said Goofy. "I'm sure I will love being a sea captain!"

The ship sailed into port, and the cargo was brought ashore. Captain Goofy sold his goods and earned a great pile of gold coins. That night he ate dinner with the finest men and women in town. He ordered soup and fish

and steak and cake. Goofy had never eaten so well! While he ate, he told his new friends about his adventures at sea and all the money he had made as a ship's captain.

After dinner, Captain Goofy laid down on his soft bed and went to sleep. But Goofy had talked too much at dinner about his gold coins. Word had spread around town, and soon two robbers showed up at Goofy's window. While he slept, they crawled into his room and stole all his money. They even stole his new parrot!

When Goofy woke up, he saw that all of his things were missing. With no gold, Goofy could not stay at the inn any longer. So once again, he rowed out to sea.

"Magic fish! Magic fish!" Goofy called. "Come up and help your poor friend."

Soon the magic fish appeared. "Are you back so soon?" it asked. "What is it that you wish for now?"

"I wish to be a king. Kings never have any problems," Goofy replied.

Poof!

The next thing he knew, Goofy was sitting on a throne with a crown on his head. All around him stood servants and townsfolk. Knights bowed deeply to King Goofy, and musicians played his favorite songs.

"Finally I have chosen the right thing," said Goofy. "I am sure I will like being a king!"

But a few days later, one of King Goofy's guards interrupted him as he was eating his breakfast.

"Your Majesty!" he shouted. "The soldiers are refusing to ride out and protect the kingdom!"

"Refusing? But they must do as I say," said King Goofy. "I must see what is happening!"

King Goofy hurried up the stairs to the tallest tower in the castle. But when he looked out the window, he grew very frightened. On the other side of the castle's moat stood his entire royal army.

"We want a new king!" shouted the knights.

"A new king?" said Goofy. "But I have not done anything!"

As the soldiers continued to shout, Goofy realized that maybe the reason they were angry was *because* he had done nothing. He had let them do all the work of the kingdom!

King Goofy ran away from the castle and out to the beach as quickly as his royal legs could carry him. Down by the water, King Goofy found a small rowboat and paddled out to sea.

"Magic fish! Magic fish!" he called. "Come up and help your poor friend."

Soon the magic fish appeared. "What is wrong, Goofy? Do you not like being a king?" it asked.

"Being a king is dangerous!" Goofy replied. "I wish I were a fisherman again. At least then I knew I was safe."

Poof!

With a puff of smoke, Goofy found himself back at his small house by the water. Goofy sat in his rocking chair and looked out at the sea.

"That is much better," he said. "I think I will enjoy being a fisherman after all."

From that day on, Goofy was happy. And he never called on the magic fish again.